SNOOPY'S
Two-Minute Stories

Peanuts® characters created and drawn by CHARLES M. SCHULZ

Text by JUSTINE KORMAN
Background illustrations by ART and KIM ELLIS

A GOLDEN BOOK • NEW YORK
Western Publishing Company, Inc., Racine, Wisconsin 53404

It's a Dog's Life

One day, as Snoopy trotted behind the Peanuts gang on their way to school, Linus said, "Snoopy is so lucky. I wish I were a dog."

Charlie Brown agreed. "Dogs don't have to go to school or anything. It must be great to be a dog."

"Ha!" thought Snoopy. "They don't know how tough my life is!"

When the kids got home from school that day, Snoopy knew he was right. No one wanted to play baseball with a dog, or marbles or draughts. Snoopy wasn't any good at hopscotch, and he certainly couldn't play the piano like Schroeder.

When Snoopy tried to get a lick off Lucy's ice-cream cone, she screamed, "Dog germs!" and ran away.

"It's a dog's life," Snoopy said sadly.

From his doghouse Snoopy could see Charlie Brown being knocked out of his socks on the pitcher's mound.

After the baseball game, Snoopy saw Charlie Brown build a sand castle. As soon as he finished the castle, Lucy kicked it down.

After that, Charlie Brown tried to fly his kite. It never got off the ground, but the string went everywhere. Charlie Brown ended up tied to a tree.

Then it was time for Charlie Brown to do his homework. Snoopy stared at the maths problems until his head started to spin.

After he finished his homework, Charlie Brown had to clean his room and set the table for dinner. Snoopy was beginning to think that being a dog wasn't so bad after all.

"Work, work, work," Charlie Brown grumbled. "That's all I ever do around here. Take out the garbage, feed the dog..."

"Feed the dog?" Snoopy thought. "It's suppertime!" Snoopy ran in happy circles around Charlie Brown's feet.

Snoopy settled down to a delicious dinner. "It's too bad everyone isn't lucky enough to be a dog!" he thought.

Chasing Rainbows

One day after a rainstorm, the sun came out and there was a beautiful rainbow. Snoopy and Woodstock admired the rainbow until it faded away.

Snoopy and Woodstock were very sad. Where did the rainbow go? they wondered. Snoopy grabbed his detective hat and magnifying glass. He set off with his trusty assistant to find the rainbow and bring it back.

Detective Snoopy and Woodstock searched high and low, but they didn't find a trace of the missing rainbow. What they did find was Lucy giving Linus a science lesson.

"You see," Lucy began in a serious voice, "a rainbow is the coloured smoke that comes from elf planes streaking through the sky."

"Then why do we only see rainbows after it rains?" Linus asked.

"Because elf planes use raindrops as fuel, so they can only fly..." Lucy's voice trailed off.

"What is it, Charlie Brown?" she asked. "Why are you moaning and banging your head against that tree?"

"Because I just can't stand it when you tell Linus all those dumb things!" Charlie Brown shouted.

"What dumb things?" Lucy asked.

"Like elf planes causing rainbows," Charlie Brown said. "A rainbow is the sun's rays reflected in the mist left after it rains. That's why you only see rainbows after a rainstorm, or over a waterfall, where the air is full of mist."

Detective Snoopy put down his magnifying glass and smiled at his trusty assistant. Their search was over. The mystery was solved. The rainbow wasn't gone forever. There would be a bright new rainbow after the next rainstorm.

Fun Is Where You Find It

It was summertime and most of the Peanuts gang were going away on vacation. Schroeder was off to music camp. Lucy and Linus were going to visit relatives. Marcie and Peppermint Patty were going to sleep-away camp.

"Good-bye, Snoopy!" they all shouted. "See you in the autumn!"

Snoopy and Woodstock waved sadly until everyone was gone.

Woodstock chirped at Snoopy. It just wasn't fair that everyone else was going to have so much fun this summer.

"We should go somewhere, too," Snoopy decided.

They put all their money together and counted it. There wasn't even enough money for bus fare into town. Snoopy felt discouraged, and the hot sun was making him thirsty. Suddenly he had an idea!

LeMONADE
5¢ a glass

"We'll open a lemonade stand," he told Woodstock. "Then we'll earn enough money to go on vacation!"

Snoopy and Woodstock worked hard. They built their stand on the side of a busy road and sold pink lemonade to everyone who drove by.

Still Snoopy wasn't satisfied. He wanted more customers, more lemonade, more money! He built a giant billboard for the highway, with a flashing neon arrow to point the way to the stand. Snoopy put lights up all around the stand and kept it open twenty-four hours a day.

Soon Woodstock was so tired, he fell asleep stirring a pitcher of lemonade and dropped right in. Snoopy was so busy, he didn't even notice as he poured Woodstock into a cup.

Woodstock jumped out of the cup and shook his feathers furiously.

"If you quit, I quit!" Snoopy shouted.

Woodstock and Snoopy took apart the stand and counted up their profits, which weren't very much after paying for the billboard and the neon arrow.

Once again Snoopy felt very discouraged. This time Woodstock came up with an idea. He decorated Snoopy's house with flowers and a palm tree and put up a sign that said, "Club Snoopy—Luxury Resort." Then he filled Charlie Brown's paddling pool and set a deck chair beside it.

Woodstock chirped calypso music while Snoopy sipped leftover lemonade by the pool.

"What a great vacation," Snoopy said. "With enough imagination, you can go anywhere!"

Things That Go Bump in the Night

One day Snoopy and his Beagle Scouts went hiking to a campsite on the top of a mountain. They unpacked, then laid out their bedrolls. After a quick swim, they gathered wood for a campfire. As the troop cooked their dinners over a crackling fire, they watched as the fireflies gave way to the stars.

The Beagle Scouts chirped at Snoopy to tell them ghost stories.

"There is no such thing as a ghost," Scout Leader Snoopy replied. "Besides, if I tell ghost stories, you'll be too scared to sleep."

But the Beagle Scouts didn't think they would be scared. They didn't stop chirping until Snoopy gave in.

So Snoopy told the scouts ghost stories. He told the one about the haunted old mansion, and the ghost in the gooseberry patch story. He remembered the time his brother saw a ghost in the desert. And each time Snoopy finished a story the scouts begged for one more.

Finally a yawn spread around the campfire. One by one the scouts fell asleep in their teeny sleeping bags.

At last everyone was asleep—except Snoopy, who was wide awake thinking about ghosts! Snoopy stared into the darkness. Crickets chirped, frogs croaked, and...what was that?

Snoopy hid under the covers and wondered if there really were ghosts after all. He listened and listened. Whatever it was didn't sound like a ghost. It rustled and crackled like wrappers and paper bags.

Suddenly Snoopy realized what was happening. He jumped out of his sleeping bag and ran toward the backpack full of food supplies. But on the way Snoopy tripped on a root and fell into the clothesline. A wet white towel fell over his head.

"Ow!" Snoopy howled from the pain in his toe, and he wrestled with the wet towel stuck on his head.

The noise woke the Beagle Scouts, who screeched when they saw Snoopy.

"No, it's not a ghost! It's only me," Snoopy said, dropping the towel. "Look!" he added, pointing to a bushy tail disappearing into the woods. "It was a raccoon trying to get our food," he explained. "Your screams must have scared him away." Woodstock and the other scouts still looked very frightened.

"There are no ghosts!" Snoopy said firmly.

But somehow no one wanted to sleep alone that night. The troop bundled into Snoopy's big sleeping bag. They snuggled under the covers, but they were still too frightened to sleep.

"I'm going to tell you a story about something nice," Snoopy said. "Then you won't have nightmares."

The scouts huddled together. Maybe Snoopy's story was about a bear—or even a lion!

"It's about something that's going to happen very soon," Snoopy said with a yawn. "Once upon a time there was a breakfast..."

Judge for Yourself

When Snoopy heard about the dog show coming to town, he could hardly wait to win. What other dog was a World War I Flying Ace, or the World's Greatest Author?

Charlie Brown tried to explain that these dog show judges weren't looking for talent or personality. They gave prizes to the dogs with the best breeding and form.

Lucy laughed. "You can't win a dog show," she sneered. "You're a disobedient mutt!"

"I am not a mutt!" Snoopy thought. He was more determined than ever to enter and win!

On the day of the show Snoopy watched the other dogs walk quietly into the ring. They were all well groomed, with papers to prove their pure breeding. They all posed perfectly for the judges.

But the crowd went wild when Snoopy did his tricks.

"How original!" someone shouted.

"Plenty of spirit," one of the judges remarked.

When it came time to give out the prizes, Snoopy's chest swelled with pride. Here was the moment!

"First prize goes to..."

A bulldog marched past Snoopy on his way to the winner's platform. Snoopy stared in disbelief as a poodle pranced by to take second prize. Third place went to a pampered Pekingese.

"He doesn't even do tricks!" Snoopy thought disgustedly.

Snoopy dragged himself home with his tail between his legs. When he got near his doghouse, Snoopy looked up in surprise. The house was covered with ribbons that said, "Best Dog," "Magnificent Friend," and even "Snoopy for President."

"Surprise!" the Peanuts gang shouted.

"We wanted you to know that we think you're the best dog in the world," Charlie Brown said.

"We know you better than those dog show judges," said Linus.

"And we still love you!" Lucy added.

Then before Lucy could stop him, Snoopy kissed her right on the nose.

It's Hard to Say Good-bye

When Snoopy saw the circus, he thought that was the life for him.
"Maybe I'll be a clown," he said, "or learn how to walk a tightrope, or
swing through the air on the flying trapeze."

So he packed his things and went to say good-bye to all his friends.
Woodstock gave Snoopy a tail feather to remember him by. Linus pulled
out a thread from his precious blanket. Lucy whispered that she would miss
him. Schroeder gave Snoopy a Beethoven record. Sally made him promise
to write, even if it was only a paw print.

But Charlie Brown's good-bye was the hardest of all.

"I'll miss you every day," Charlie Brown said. "I'll never get another dog, and I'll keep your house just as you left it so you can always come home."

Charlie Brown started to cry. Then Snoopy burst into tears. He was homesick already.

"If you don't really want to go, why don't you stay?" Linus asked. Snoopy blinked, and Charlie Brown looked at him hopefully.

Snoopy unpacked his bag and climbed back onto his doghouse. Home, sweet home was harder to leave than he thought.

And May the Best Friend Win

One day Woodstock signed up for a talent contest. Woodstock asked if he could borrow Snoopy's "Boogie Woogie Beagle Boy" record so he could sing the song in the contest. Snoopy lent Woodstock the record, but then he had an idea.

"I'm very talented," Snoopy thought. "I should enter the contest, too!"

Hearing Woodstock practise gave Snoopy another idea. "That 'Boogie Woogie Beagle Boy' is a catchy tune," he said. "I bet I could do a great dance number to it."

Snoopy entered the contest, and the two friends practised together. Woodstock sang and Snoopy danced. At first rehearsals were fun. Woodstock showed Snoopy a new dance step, and Snoopy tapped out the beat for his singing friend.

As the day of the contest drew near, Snoopy thought more and more about winning. He thought about how much he wanted the prize, and how upset he would be if Woodstock won instead of him. He wondered what would happen if Woodstock sang before he danced. Maybe by the time Snoopy got on stage the judges would be tired of "Boogie Woogie Beagle Boy."

"It's my record," Snoopy said to Woodstock. "I don't want you to practise with it any more."

Woodstock could hardly believe his ears. The contest was the next day, and, after all, Woodstock had entered it first.

Snoopy just picked up the record and started to walk away. Woodstock flew over and grabbed the other end of the record. They both pulled, and the record landed with a crash on the ground.

"Now look what we've done!" Snoopy wailed, but Woodstock had an idea.

The next day at the contest Woodstock and Snoopy strutted out on the stage together. Snoopy began his dance as Woodstock started to sing. When their song ended, the two friends bowed to thunderous applause.

"What a great act!" the judges exclaimed as they presented Snoopy and Woodstock with the winner's trophy.

Snoopy grabbed one handle of the trophy and Woodstock grabbed the other. They both started to tug. Just as they were about to break the trophy, Woodstock let Snoopy have it.

Snoopy realized how silly he had been. "No, you take it," he told Woodstock.

So Woodstock and Snoopy decided to share the trophy as a reminder that when friends work together, everyone wins.

Night Noises

After a long and hard battle, the World War I Flying Ace climbed wearily to the top of the barracks.

"Curse you, Red Baron!" he shouted, shaking an angry paw in the air.

It had been a rough day. Snoopy was exhausted. He closed his eyes and...

He heard the *thwack, thwack* of a baseball landing in a glove. Charlie Brown and Linus were playing catch. Lucy sang a rhyme at the top of her lungs as she skipped rope. From inside, Schroeder played Beethoven's Ninth on his piano.

How was a dog supposed to sleep with all that racket?

But as the sun faded, the games stopped.

"Good night," Charlie Brown called to his friends.

"See you tomorrow," Linus said.

Schroeder finished his symphony. Woodstock stopped chirping. The moon rose and stars twinkled in the dark sky.

Snoopy closed his eyes. It was too quiet to sleep!

Then he remembered his favourite lullaby. Snoopy smiled up at the moon and sang himself to sleep.

Sweet dreams, Snoopy!